The Happiest Moments of My Life

Jolina Böttcher

Bibliographical Information of the German National Library:
This publication is listed in the German National Bibliography of the German National Library; detailed bibliographical information can be accessed under http: //dnb.d-nb.de

Cover Design and Illustration: Marge Turingan (@caravelle_creates)

Publisher: BoD · Books on Demand GmbH, In de Tarpen 42, 22848 Norderstedt, bod@bod.de

Printing and production: Libri Plureos GmbH, Friedensallee 273, 22763 Hamburg, Germany

ISBN: 978-3-7693-0803-7

For my mother,

who always encouraged me to read.

And for Marie,

without whom this story would not have been told.

Prologue

Once upon a time, a man and a woman fell in love.

They each had been in love before. They each had been hurt by love before.

The woman had a daughter, whose father left before she was born.

The man had a son, whose mother died when he was still very young.

On the day they said their vows they meant them. They hoped that this would be the happy ending to their story.

It was not.

1

As the seat belt sign turned back on, Lorena took out her pocket mirror and readjusted her rose lipstick, before attempting to fix her bangs. Considering the long flight from New York to London, her brown hair looked still quite set.

The mirror disappeared in her purse and Lorena turned to look outside the window towards the lights, illuminating the city hundreds of meters beneath her. She found herself smiling upon the thought of being here again. It truly had been too long.

Though Lorena grew up in the United States, her mother moved them to Oxford shortly after she turned eight. It hadn´t been a pleasant experience at all. When she was younger, the kids used to make fun of her accent. When she was older, they told her how sophisticated it made her sound and loved the idea of having lived somewhere else entirely.

Lorena did not care much either way. It was something she had learned from her mother very early – to stand above things and focus on what mattered. And to her, that was her friendship with Jack.

She hadn´t liked the idea of a stepbrother very much at first. She would have preferred a sister. Someone she could dress up with and who could give her advice on things she didn´t want to ask her mom about.

But then Lorena had met Jack and once she got to know him, she wouldn´t have traded him for any sister in the world. Oh, the getting to know him part wasn´t that easy. Jack wasn´t as extroverted as she was. He could be content with locking himself up in his room, reading about and playing chess for hours, getting totally lost in his own world.

In time he opened up to her and they grew close. It was because of this that the divorce of their parents felt like the end of the world. At the ages of ten and twelve, life was hard enough without having to lose one's best friend. Still, the divorce happened, and Lorena's mother moved back to the US with her, before returning to England six years later.

Coming back then had been strange, knowing nobody was waiting to pick them up. It was starting new all over again and even though Lorena had accepted it, she hadn't been eager to step off the plane that day. Other than now, where she had to force herself to remain calm and not jump off her seat as soon as the plane landed. She waited patiently, as the passengers passed by her to exit before she grabbed her stuff and followed them outside.

While standing in line to get her passport checked, Lorena pulled out her phone and turned the flight mode off. Unread messages came stumbling in, but she didn't open any of them. Instead, she clicked on Jack's name and typed: *Landed*. Then she slipped her phone back into her purse and moved to the front of the line.

The airport was relatively empty, but still full considering the time on a Friday evening. It had been already dark outside when Jack had pulled his car into the parking lot and now the white-blue light of the ceiling lamps seemed terribly bright.

He pulled his phone out of his pocket and checked for new messages. The flight from New York had landed half an hour ago, but Jack rather suspected that after passport control, Lorena still had to wait for her suitcase. It was one of the things he usually avoided. The few times he had flown over to the US to visit her, he had managed to fit everything into a small suitcase that qualified as carry-on baggage. Lorena was only staying until Sunday, but somehow she would manage to pack enough stuff to change into three different outfits every day.

Jack didn´t even try to stifle a laugh, as he saw her from afar, pushing a suitcase beside her, which was almost half her size. She was wearing black trousers and a white blouse, being probably the only person who had bothered to dress up for an eight-hour flight, which would reach its destination around 9 pm. But it was just how she was. She always looked pretty and in style, in a simple, elegant kind of way.

Lorena noticed him and waved. Jack raised an eyebrow at her luggage to which she just shrugged before breaking into a wide grin.

"Didn´t know you were coming to live with me", Jack said, embracing her in a tight hug, lifting her off the floor and making her laugh in surprise.

"You wish", she said, as she was standing on her feet again. "One week and you´d be running for the hills!"

The warm feeling still circled in his chest and Jack cleared his throat, resisting the urge to pull her into another hug. "Ready?"

"Sure."

They made their way towards the exit and onto the parking lot, where the old green Audi 80 B4 was parked, which Jack had gotten after college graduation. His dad had wanted to gift him a new car, but Jack had wanted to buy his first car himself. His friends back then had declared him insane for wasting money on that old thing. Then, however, Jack had to admit that the guys he had hung out with in college had been idiots.

"For you", he said, once they had taken their seats and handed Lorena the cup of tea he had brought for her.

"Thank you." She took a little sip and placed her chin on top of the lid.

"There is a pillow on the back too, in case you want to rest."

A corner of her mouth curved up. "Tired of me already? You are aware though that London is ahead of New York, right?"

Jack fixed his seat belt. "Just thinking of your beauty sleep. Plane rides can be exhausting."

"Flattered, but unnecessary." She sat straighter, lifting her chin. "I look naturally lovely."

"If you say so."

Jack started to laugh as she gave him a friendly punch with the elbow, then he started the engine, set the car back, and drove out of the parking lot.

While Jack was driving, Lorena leaned back in her seat, letting her gaze slide outside the window. It would take them two hours to get to Oxford, maybe less, since the streets were empty. A bus passed by on what was – at least for her - the wrong side of the road and she found herself smiling. She had missed her second home. She turned to look at Jack, whose eyes were fixed on the street. She had missed him too.

Jack caught her gaze. "What?"

Since leaving for college when she was 18 years old, Lorena and Jack had only managed to visit each other a couple of times within the last eight years. It had gotten better once both of them had graduated, but they rarely saw each other more than once a year.

"Nothing", she said, still smiling, but feeling her heart ache all of a sudden.

Jack shot her a side glance, a short strand of dark hair falling into his face before he had to focus on the street again. Lorena looked at him for a few more seconds, then she turned her head towards the window.

Life did take unexpected turns sometimes indeed.

"I´m supposed to say hi from my dad to you, by the way."

"Isn´t he going to be there tomorrow?"

"No, he is in Dublin until next week."

"Pity", Lorena said and meant it. "I wanted him to fill me in on all the details of his engagement. I can´t believe he is getting married for the fourth time."

"That makes two of us."

Lorena turned her head towards him, trying to determine how he was feeling. "So, what is she like?"

"Nice, I suppose", he admitted and tapped the blinker. "I think this one might actually work out for him."

Even though they didn´t agree on everything and had quite a different character, Lorena knew how much Jack admired his father and wanted him to be happy.

"Can´t wait to meet her then", she said, and he returned the smile she gave him.

"Since we´re on the topic... Are you sure you´re okay with hanging out with my friends tomorrow?"

"Of course, I´m excited." She leaned in conspiratorially. "I have heard stories after all."

Jack didn´t take the eyes off the road to look at her. "Well, they are excited to meet you too."

"And you are not."

"You know that´s not it."

Outside Lorena could see the lights of other cars passing by in a blur, the silence inside their vehicle drawing out.

"Did you tell them?"

As she turned back to look at Jack, she could see the white of his knuckles, where his hand enclosed the steering wheel. The other arm was resting on the door frame, his fingers traveling mindlessly over the bottom of his lips.

"I told Dean", he admitted. "I´m not sure if Ava or Sonya know. I don´t suppose so."

Dean was, beside herself, Jack´s best friend. They had met when he joined the same soccer club, and Lorena knew how much it meant that he had volunteered the information. She softened. "It will be fine, Jack."

"I hope so."

"I *know* so."

She wasn´t sure if he believed her, but this time he did look at her and as he did so, she could see the corners of his lips curling up, the good humor returning to his eyes.

"I missed you."

"I missed you too."

2

Jack tied his shoelaces and shot a glance toward Lorena, who had already gone on to choose a bowling ball for him. It was a tradition, almost. Bowling on his birthday, minigolf on hers. It was what they had done with their parents in that first year they´d known each other and it somehow stuck.

The years Lorena hadn´t been there on his birthday or he hadn´t been there for hers, they had simply attended the same event individually, video chatting while doing so. It wasn´t as good as doing it together, especially since it proved to be quite an adventure to organize due to the time difference, but it was still preferable to doing anything else.

Jack had been determined to like Lorena since his father seemed to be so happy with her mother. At the beginning it had been strange, because she was so much more outgoing than him, talking and teasing the entire time. But soon he found himself laughing with her and being overcome by a feeling of belonging he hadn´t known before.

Some of his friends found it strange that he actually seemed to enjoy spending time with his new sister and others even teased him about it because she was also two years younger. And later in college, well, that had been an entirely different story altogether.

Of course that didn´t stop Jack from spending time with Lorena. But it would have been a lie to say that it didn´t put a strain on their relationship. Other than her, he took other people´s opinions to heart. He hated it, but he cared about how they saw him, how they saw her and what they said about their relationship. He wanted the people he considered his friends to like her or, at the very least, not to tease about her in inappropriate ways.

That was one of the reasons why he nowadays paid close attention to the number of times he talked about her and how he referred to her. So while his friends knew that he had a friend in America whom he was relatively close with, he usually referred to her as a childhood friend.

Jack felt horrible about it, but he was anxious about Lorena meeting his friends. Oh, he was sure they would get along great. His friends would love her. But at one point, they would ask about how they knew each other, and things would take a turn. They always did. And yet he hoped that it would be different.

The voices of his friends coming from the door forced him to get up to greet them.

"As you said we were bowling, I thought you were kidding", Ava said, managing to strike a tone that was chatty and disgusted at the same time, as she kissed him on both cheeks. "Though, I suppose, based on the amount of bowling shirts you own, I shouldn´t be."

Ava was a little intense sometimes, someone whose main reason to become a lawyer was the possibility of dressing up in stylish business clothes and getting paid for arguing with people. Still, she was funny in that way and Jack rather liked her, even though he had to admit, the main reason they became friends in the first place was because she was Dean´s twin sister.

"One never kids about bowling", Dean said, rolling his eyes at his sister, but smiling still as he embraced his best friend. "Happy birthday, Jack."

"Thanks."

Sonya hugged him next, a friendly smile on her face, as she congratulated him as well. Though she had been Dean´s girlfriend ever since Jack met him, he couldn´t say that they were very close. She worked long shifts at the hospital and often preferred to go to bed early rather than spend the evening with the rest of them.

"You really do that every year?", Sonya asked, stroking a straight dark strand of hair behind her ear and looking around. It wasn´t really the first time Jack spent his birthday with his friends, but he did tend to do evening sit-ins, after having finished his usual birthday traditions. Something he had mentioned before but had never invited them to.

"We try to."

"I must admit I´ve never played before."

Ava´s revelation wasn´t that much of a surprise. Wearing worn-out shoes, which dozens of people had worn before her and sticking her fingers into the bowling ball, which would be hard for her to disinfect didn´t really sound like something she would voluntarily do. But there was nothing – absolutely nothing – Ava loved more than a challenge.

"It´s about time then", Dean said, clapping his hands together. "You better make sure your shoes fit, because I am in for a win."

"Yeah, don´t get too excited. Lorena may be the one to beat."

She had been close enough to hear their conversation and stopped snooping through the balls, as he mentioned her name, declaring: "I am two wins ahead in bowling and four in total."

"I think you´re actually at five", Jack admitted thoughtfully, instinctively placing his hand on her back as she joined them, spinning a pink bowling ball in her hand.

"That last one doesn´t count, we didn´t even finish."

"You were so far ahead, there was no need to finish."

"I could have totally screwed up the second half of the course", Lorena insisted. "You know I always mess up the one with the net."

Jack sighed, looking down for a moment, before turning back to his other guests. "Lorena, these are my friends. Dean, Ava and Sonya."

"Nice to meet you."

"You too", Ava said, arching her eyebrows up impressively in Jack´s direction. He felt his mood darken in an instant. There was no way she would not put him on trial later.

"Well, I guess we should get some shoes then."

Jack watched them go over to the counter to get their shoes, before turning back to Lorena, who gave him a reassuring squeeze of the shoulder, as she passed by him, clearly still not content with the ball she had picked for him.

"So, boys against girls?", Ava suggested, once they were all set up. "Lorena, are you in?"

"Absolutely."

The glance she shot Jack was a challenge. He snorted and shook his head. Having her and Ava on the same team might turn out to be not such a good thing for Dean and him, but there was no way in hell he was going to make this one easy on her. "Have you made your choice?"

"Baby green."

"Baby blue."

"You are so going to lose", he said, exchanging bowling balls with her.

"We are so going to win."

Their staring contest was interrupted by Dean´s voice: "First shot, Jack, let´s go."

Even though Jack hadn´t wanted to make this an easy win for Lorena, the girls proved to be an incomparable team. It became obvious very fast that Dean and him didn´t stand a chance, but for Jack seeing all of his closest friends getting along perfectly, accepting Lorena as if she would have always been one of them, was the real win of the evening.

"So, Lorena, you´re from New York?", Sonya asked.

After finishing, they all sat down at one of the booths next to the alley, ordering milkshakes and fries.

"I am, born and raised."

"Really? That´s so cool", Ava said, leaving a red lipstick mark on her drinking straw. "I´m a total city girl at heart. I always wanted to go, but something always came up."

Lorena had no problem picturing Ava walking the streets of New York like she owned them. It was something she had never really managed. She got close to it when strolling around with her friends, but even then, it wasn´t quite right. Pushing the thought away, she smiled. "Well, if you do, let me know. We can meet up."

"You might want to reconsider that, she is a pain in the ass", Dean said, laughingly parring the jab from his sister.

Sonya, who was sitting in the corner of the booth, next to the twins, took a sip from her milkshake, attentively noting: "If you´re from New York, then how did you guys meet? Jack mentioned you were childhood friends."

At that moment, Lorena was uncommonly aware of how close Jack was sitting next to her. Relaxed at how smooth things had been going so far, his arm was placed around the back of her bench, his fingers mindlessly toying with a strand of her hair. There was a small flicker in her smile, as she hesitated for the blink of a second, but her voice sounded normal as she answered: "Our parents used to be married."

It took a few moments for her words to sink in. Lorena saw both Sonya's and Ava's eyes move from her to Jack, whose body slightly tensed beside her as he locked gazes with his best friend.

"Wait a second..." Ava leaned forward. "So, your mother and your father were... married. Like married, married?"

"Yeah, they were together for like two to three years in total", Jack said, clearing his throat and turning to look at Ava instead of Dean. "Little break in between."

"My mom moved back with me to America after the divorce and got back shortly before Jack was to leave for college", Lorena added. "They met again by chance and thus the second act of their romance began. Lasted only a few months though."

"And you guys stayed friends", Sonya concluded and the smile she had on her face seemed genuine. "That´s really sweet actually."

"Thanks", Lorena said, her smile beginning to falter. She started sensing the awkwardness that settled upon them but joined in on Sonya's attempt to keep a conversation, nonetheless. "We barely see each other though. I moved back to America for college and stayed there."

"You might try to look a little less shocked", Dean suggested to his sister.

"Well, I am shocked", Ava exclaimed. "I genuinely thought Jack kept a girlfriend from us. You guys could have totally convinced me you were secretly dating. He isn´t that comfortable with anyone."

"Well, I am not comfortable now."

"I´m sorry", she said, visibly making an effort to calm herself. "I didn´t mean to make a big deal out of it. I just... did not see this one coming."

"Well, we have known each other for 18 years", Lorena pointed out. "I think it´s safe to say that we are relatively close."

"And I can´t even judge you, because I hang out with this guy voluntarily all the time", Ava said, waving her hand toward her brother.

"That is true, even though I could have sworn you once told me that you couldn´t wait to be finally rid of me. In fact, I think you told me that more than once."

"When we were kids." Ava rolled her eyes. "Who could have known you were so resentful?"

"That did go rather well, don´t you think?", Lorena said, sweeping her arms through his. They left the bowling alley behind them, starting the walk to his apartment.

"It did", Jack agreed. After the short discussion over the topic of their relationship, they had moved on from it and spent another hour talking and laughing before they decided that it was getting rather late. He didn´t even try to hide the smile on his face.

There was a small nudge in his side.

"I told you so."

The smile went wider, and he pulled his arm from hers, to wrap it around her shoulders.

"You did."

They continued walking in companionable silence. Lorena let her head fall against his shoulder and he turned his head, inhaling the scent of her shampoo as he pulled her closer. A wave of contentment washed over him and instead of suppressing the tingling in his chest, for once, he embraced it.

"You know", Lorena said eventually, as they reached a traffic light. There wasn´t a single car to be seen and Jack would have probably walked on, but he knew that she had a different opinion on the matter of traffic safety and since stopping meant holding her for a couple of seconds more, he didn´t complain. "I don´t mind the traffic thing when I´m in a car, but it is confusing with the correct side of the sidewalk."

"Nobody pays attention to who walks on the correct side of the *pavement*", Jack argued, putting a deliberate emphasis on the last word. From the corner of his eyes, he could see her lips twitch. "You´ve got to admit, it´s the prettier word."

"It´s the *side* of the road and we *walk* on it. Therefore, it is a *sidewalk*", Lorena countered. "It´s descriptive. And practical."

The points of argument felt reversed, and Jack snorted as a memory popped into his head. "This reminds me of the times we used to make presentations and had our parents vote on the superior words."

"Oh god."

"I think I still have the list somewhere."

With his free hand, he reached to tug a strand of hair out of her face.

"And I think that we actually tied on the... sidewalk thing."

Lorena's breath caught, as his fingers accidentally brushed her cheek. Jack was aware that the smart thing to do would be to drop his hand, but he hesitated. His heart beat louder by the second, as he let his thumb trace the soft skin of her cheek down to and over the bottom of her lip. All he wanted to do was lean in and kiss her.

The traffic light turned green, the accompanying beeping tone waking Jack from his trance. He cleared his throat and let his hand drop, not looking at her. "It´s green."

The words had barely left his lips when the color changed back to red.

"Let´s just go", Lorena quietly suggested and started to walk, his arm sliding off her shoulder.

3

The number of people traveling on regular days never failed to amaze Jack, as he was standing in the airport hall with Lorena, facing having to say goodbye even though he would have wanted her to stay. The admission was both a natural and unsettling thought, neither of which he felt like analyzing.

After leaving the bowling alley yesterday, they hadn´t talked much before going to bed and Jack had been overcome by the feeling that they were drifting apart from each other. When they video-chatted or called, it was easy enough to ignore, as with the distance between them of course he felt like she was too far away, living another life parallel to his own, really. But in the last years, whenever they saw each other, sooner or later it had become obvious that no matter how much they cared, one day things would turn and there was nothing he could do about it.

Jack glanced at Lorena, who, despite the early hour, looked like she was more likely to be taking a spring stroll rather than a multi-hour flight. She was checking her phone, not looking up while studying the airline´s website for updates on her flight. She furrowed her brows in a thoughtful expression he had memorized as well as he had everything else about her. The familiarity tucked at him in this slightly painful way that he had grown too used to lately.

When he had gotten up this morning, the other side of the bed had been cold, and the sound of the shower running had come from the adjacent room. He had tried to brush off the mood from the day before, knowing very well he would regret it if they were to spend the precious few hours they had left in some sort of strange tension. Not that he had to worry about it. When Lorena joined him in the kitchen, she sat down with him, and after taking her teabag out of her cup, she looked at him and reached for his hand to squeeze it. Jack returned the gesture, a little more confident than he had felt moments before.

The drive back to London Airport they spent in pleasant silence. When the time came for Jack to say goodbye, he pulled her in an embrace, closing his eyes and holding her close. Pulling back a little, he tried to smile, brushing a strand of hair out of her face, allowing his thumb to brush her cheek. He hated to watch her leave.

"See you soon?"

"Of course."

They didn´t embrace again and as she turned to leave, he felt his heart break, feelings of regret already pulling at him. Resisting the urge to leap forward, grab her arm and ask her to stay, his feet stayed planted on the ground and he waved goodbye, as she turned one last time, smiling halfheartedly, unconvincingly, before vanishing from his life again.

4

5 years ago

Jack watched with a mixture of amusement and skepticism as Lorena emptied her glass in one go, signaling the barkeeper to give her a refill.

"Just because you are allowed to drink alcohol now doesn´t mean you have to overdo it."

"You´re just scared I could out-drink you." She ignored the snorting sound he made and sat up a little bit straighter, raising her glass to toast. "I only turn 21 once."

"I´ll drink to that", Jack said, joining in on her laughter as they toasted, before emptying their shot glasses in one go.

Jack grimaced and pressed his fingers to his mouth, while Lorena shook her head as if she could get rid of the bitter taste this way. Then their eyes met.

"Want to take a walk?"

"Great idea."

Jack helped Lorena get into her jacket and opened the door for her, as they left the bar.

"I have to admit, I was surprised that you didn´t throw a grand party."

"You flew all the way for one weekend just to be there on my birthday. I´m not going to throw a party where I have to fuss over some random people the entire time."

"I´m flattered."

It was Lorena's turn to snort then, causing the corners of Jack´s mouth to pull up. As they walked in silence, Lorena pulled her jacket closer before her chest, her eyes focused ahead.

"I miss you."

The words in itself probably weren´t surprising, but they felt like an admission to feelings she didn´t know how to name.

"I miss you too."

Lorena glanced up at him and as their eyes met, it looked for a moment like Jack was thinking about kissing her. Then he managed to look away, clearing his throat: "We should see each other more often."

Lorena tried to sort out her confused feelings, but she had a hard time banning the tingling feeling in her chest from her body. "Well, I guess it´s good I´m also out of college soon."

"You still have one year to go."

And like that, the conversation and their lives continued as if this moment had never happened.

5

After almost eight hours on the plane, Lorena landed in New York in the early evening local time. It took her almost another two hours to claim her luggage, get a cap and arrive at her apartment. Rolling her suitcase through the door, her phone started ringing in her purse.

"Managed to get home okay?"

Jack´s face appeared on her screen. His hair looked disheveled, as if he was already half asleep and Lorena's heart skipped a beat at the look of it.

"Yeah", she said, thinking of the five-hour time difference between Oxford and New York. "No need to call, you should be asleep."

"Kind of already am."

Lorena smiled softly. "Go to sleep, we´ll talk tomorrow."

"Night, Lorena."

"Night, Jack."

The call disconnected. Even though they had said their goodbyes already today, it felt like letting go all over. Lorena felt her smile falter, as she sank onto her couch.

Maybe letting go wasn´t the right word. Maybe it was just the feeling that this place she lived in wasn´t her home and never would feel like it, not in the way that Jack´s place did. It wasn´t even the space itself. It looked good, though modern and minimalistic had always been more of her mother´s preferred taste, which she only took on because it was easy to take care of. Lorena had always preferred Jack´s thrown-together flat. She was, however, willing to admit that that was the result of the comfort he gave her and not of the interior design style.

Lonely. She was lonely. Not alone, of course. It was not like Lorena didn´t have any friends. She had maintained a group of friends from college, with whom she regularly went to have drinks, and she got along great with her colleagues at work. But at the end of the day, Jack was the person she felt closest to, despite the distance. And every time she had to leave him again, she felt a piece of herself fading away.

While everything in her longed to spend the evening at home, drowning in her own negative emotions, when she read the text in the group chat asking to go out for drinks, she only hesitated a moment before confirming. Getting out of her head seemed to be a good idea.

"Sorry, guys", Jenn said, as she shrugged off her raincoat. "Missed my metro."

"Even Lorena managed to get here on time, and she flew in just a few hours ago", Francis noted, making room on the bench for her anyway.

"Was it as rainy as it is here?"

Lorena laughed. "It was fine."

She had met Jenn, Francis and Barb in her first year of college, as they had been assigned to the same dorm and somehow, they had stuck together ever since. Even though life had taken them in different directions, they always got back together.

"Here." Barb pushed a glass over to Jenn. "We already ordered for you."

"Thanks, B", she said, brushing a wet blonde strand of her out of her face.

Except for Lorena, they all had nicknames – Jenn for Jennifer, Barb or B for Barbara, Fran for Francis – but none of the ones they had thought up for Lorena had ever stuck.

"Well." Barb raised her glass. "To us!"

"To us!"

The glasses clinked together, and the girls started to giggle, as Jenn choked on her drink and spit out half of it. "That´s not funny!"

"It´s kind of funny."

"So, how is Jack?", Francis asked, after passing Jenn a napkin. "It was his birthday, right?"

"He´s fine", Lorena said, diverting her attention from Jenn to her. "We went Bowling with his friends. I flew over Friday evening."

"And got back today? That´s not long."

"Well, I have work."

"Yeah, but... I don´t see why you don´t take a week or so off to see him", Jenn said. "Only making short trips must be exhausting for both of you."

"I have done that."

It had been a long time ago though and when thinking about it, all she could recall was how the duration of each other´s visits had shortened over time while the periods of not seeing each other had grown longer.

It wasn´t that they couldn´t time their free days. It was that every time they went to see each other, it was getting harder to go.

From the corner of her eye, Lorena could see Barb signaling at Jenn discretely to drop the topic, while Francis´s glance wasn´t as friendly.

They meant well, all of them, but Lorena was glad nonetheless when Jenn relented, reaching for her glass to take a sip, not pursuing the issue.

"Anyway", Barb said. "Have I told you about the newest idea of team building my idiot of a boss has come up with?"

Lorena was grateful for the change in topic and laughed along as Barb started to tell the story in that lively way of hers, but her mind went to the first time her friends had ever met Jack, back in their third year of college when he had visited for her 21st birthday. The girls had wanted to take her out, but she had turned them down every time they offered. Lorena had mentioned Jack on multiple occasions throughout the time, giving the girls time and reason for speculation. There was some teasing, everyone was sure they had a crush on each other. Lorena didn´t like to think about her visit to Jack`s college in detail. Maybe the comments should have bothered her more in that context, but she barely acknowledged them. It wasn´t until she got home that night, that she finally told her friends how they were related, shutting down their romantic assumptions the way she knew the truth would. From then on, they let the topic rest. It wasn´t weird in the sense that they were disregarding them like Jack´s college friends were, but there was a look passed whenever he was mentioned. Lorena had long since given up on interpreting what the exchanged glances meant and started to avoid the topic unless being asked.

"Lorena?"

She blinked, being snapped out of her thoughts. "Mhm?"

Barb looked like she wanted to say something, but in the end, she settled for: "Are you okay?"

The problem wasn´t that Lorena had thought Jack might kiss her. The problem was that she had wanted him to. She still did.

"Yeah", she said, raising her glass to her lips and smiling. "Of course."

6

All this mess started in Jack´s second year of college. His dad and Lorena´s mum had broken up again a little over a year before and he hadn´t seen her since. They had texted on the occasions of holidays and birthdays, but hadn´t rekindled the friendship they had had as kids. Jack was sitting at his desk, writing an essay, as his phone binged. As he looked at it, Lorena´s name appeared on the screen.

My mum just got engaged to stepdad number five.

Jack raised his eyebrows as he typed a response.

Seriously?

The answer came directly.

Yes – they met at some company dinner a few months ago.

In regard to love and marriage, Lorena´s mother was an even greater wild card than Jack´s dad, who had married three times during the 20 years Jack had lived.

I thought she would be at husband number four?

She is, the answer read, *do you have a minute?*

For a moment Jack hesitated. The clock read 10.03 pm.

Sure.

His phone started ringing a few seconds later. After the phone exchange Jack knew that after husband three, his dad, Lorena´s mum had been together and engaged with stepdad number four for almost two years before their breakup caused them to move back to England again, making the next fiancé the soon-to-be stepdad number five. But what he remembered was her laugh, how easily comfortable he was with her and how he missed both of that. He was also surprised to learn that Lorena´s mother had not moved them back to the US after the new split, but that they had decided to stay in London until Lorena graduated.

The next day, during one of his lectures he wrote: *I feel like my prof thinks he is some kind of Beethoven in programming.*

Shortly after the lecture was over, his phone notified him of a new message: *Please elaborate.*

And from then on, their conversations just continued.

7

Jack and his father were sitting on the terrace of his small country estate, the sun breaking through the terrace beams which were entwined by all kinds of plants and flowers neither Jack nor Soraya, soon-to-be stepmom number three, could remember how to name.

"Soraya gifted me a bleeding-heart flower", Jack's father said, nodding towards a potted plant at the end of the terrace and chuckling, as he leaned back in his chair. "She said it looked pretty enough and as I told her about the name, she told me a heart could also cry for joy if I had to find some sort of meaning in it."

The first time Jack had met Soraya, they had been sitting here as well, his father, Ted, flourishing in explaining the newest addition to his garden, the way he always did when someone visited. Jack had glanced over to Soraya then, a woman in a business dress with perfectly curled dark hair, listening patiently the same way Jack tended to do – with an appreciation for his father's passion, but with the information going in on one ear and out the other. She had glanced back at Jack, a look of understanding passing between them, before she had to turn, agreeing to something her boyfriend had said about the plant next to the terrace door, but she had barely heard. "Yes, very lovely darling." The dubious glance Ted had thrown at her had made her laugh and pet his shoulder reassuringly. "It is, but I don't understand half of what you're saying. But I'm happy that you're happy." There had still been a glint of humor in her voice, but she had meant it, and Jack had known that for his father, she had to be the One.

His thoughts were interrupted by the voice of his father asking about his birthday.

"It was good."

"How long did Lorena stay?"

While Jack had never quite managed to bond with Lorena´s mother, Lorena and his father had hit it off immediately, which he supposed had something to do with how naturally she had welcomed Ted to fill the father role in her life.

"Just the weekend", Jack said, shifting in his seat. "She had to go back to work. I´m supposed to greet and congratulate you. She was kind of sad that she didn´t get to see you."

"Tell her thanks. I would have liked to see her too, it really has been a long time", Ted sighed, genuinely upset. "Actually, that is something I wanted to talk to you about."

"Okay?"

"I figured maybe she could be your plus one to the wedding."

Jack wasn´t quite what was considered conventionally attractive. He had always been the tall, lanky type with a long head that actually wasn´t that long but seemed to be that way because his eyes were so close together. It had taken him years to find a haircut that seemed to look good on him, one that didn´t highlight his standing-off ears. At the very least, his braces had done their job.

Jack had known Lorena for more than half his life and naturally, they were really close. He was comfortable with her in a way he wasn´t with any other people. The easy way he talked to her, the physical signs of affection he showed – both things he otherwise wasn´t great at, he stopped noticing around her.

From appearance, no one would mistake Lorena and him for a couple, but when they stood right next to each other, it seemed to be the most natural thought. Jack was aware of that. He knew Lorena was aware of it and somehow, while looking over the table, he supposed his father was aware of it too.

"I´m not sure if I can ask her to fly in", Jack said eventually.

But of course, he could, they both knew that. As well as they both knew that she would come if he did indeed ask.

"Just think about it", his father said.

"Wouldn´t that be awkward for Soraya?"

"Well, we are talking about Lorena, not her mother." He set his teacup down. "And she is your best and eldest friend, isn´t she?"

Jack was spared having to answer, because his father´s attention was diverted to Soraya, entering the garden through the side door.

"Ah, there she is!"

"What are you two talking about?", Soraya asked, placing a hand on her fiancée´s shoulder.

"Wedding, actually", Ted said, responding to the intimacy by pulling her towards his side in a one-armed embrace. "I just told Jack he should bring Lorena as his plus one."

Soraya shifted her attention to him. "I didn´t know you had a girlfriend."

Jack gazed at his father for a second, before he cleared his throat.

"She´s my best friend, actually", he clarified. "She lives in the US though."

"Oh, that´s a pity. Do you think she would fly in?"

"Probably."

"Jack is just hesitant because Lorena is the daughter of my third wife and he doesn´t want to upset you", his father said, ignoring the glance Jack shot him.

"Well, that is very considerate of you, Jack", Soraya amended, saying pretty much what he had thought she would say, "but there is no need."

While Lorena was still wearing her office clothes as she had barely gotten back from work, Jack was already wearing his pajamas, the kitchen only being illuminated by his laptop screen and the light above the stovetop.

"Didn´t you go to see your dad today?", Lorena asked a few minutes into the conversation.

"I did. We talked about the wedding majorly."

"That´s in a few weeks already, right?"

"Three", Jack confirmed, the admission making him even more nervous about what he was going to say next. "About that... I was wondering if you would consider coming?"

Lorena stopped venturing through her kitchen cabinets. "To the wedding?"

"Dad suggested you could be my plus one. I think he would really like to see you... and set us up."

Lorena paused for a moment. "Well, what do you think about it?"

Jack hesitated as well, before settling for the less complicated interpretation of the question. "I would like to see you, of course. It´s not a problem for Soraya. We asked and she is totally fine with it."

The expression on her face was hard to read. It made him anxious, triggering the thought that she might decide not to come.

"So?", Jack asked, hating how childishly expectant he sounded. "What do you say?"

"Well, yes", she laughed, adding an eye roll. "Obviously. I need to see if I can get off work though."

"Of course. The wedding is on a Friday. Maybe you could come a few days early, make it less hectic."

As the best man, Jack would have to help with preparations, but the idea of having Lorena around for more than just one or two days, even amidst all the wedding chaos, was a welcome thought.

"Sounds good", she agreed, leaning back from the screen and going back to preparing her dinner. "I´ll see if I can take the week off. Otherwise, I´ll just work mobile."

They stayed on the phone for a couple more minutes, before Lorena finished cooking and Jack went to bed, having to get up early tomorrow. After crawling under his blanket, he lay awake, staring at the ceiling, trying to sort his thoughts.

8

Lorena wasn´t very excited about prom, but she had gone dress shopping with her friends to humor them. They had very openly accepted her into their friend group, and she usually had a good time with them, but she wasn´t able to get herself to share their excitement about their school dance. It was odd, because she liked to wear pretty dresses and had attended every prom back at her American high school. Perhaps it was her lack of a date, even though that had also never bothered her before. It was actually how she liked it – just her and her friends, not having to be polite with someone she usually didn´t spend time with.

"I like it", Jack said honestly, as she showed him the dress on their video call later that day. "Are you excited?"

"Don´t know. My friends are."

"Are you going with them?"

"Yeah, even though...", she hesitated, making the question leave her lips before she was able to back out. "I was wondering if you would go with me?" The words were met with silence, as she caught him off guard. "I mean, it takes place on a Friday. I figured maybe you would consider coming to London for the weekend?"

They had barely seen each other in person since Jack had headed off for college. They had only started talking regularly a couple of months back and between school and finals, Lorena only has had the time to meet up with Jack twice. And now, she would be leaving soon herself. College in America had been an obvious choice. Her mother was moving back, Lorena had spent most of her life there and therefore, she had always seen her life there. Well, she had been quite happy with envisioning her life in Oxford, back when her mother and Jack´s dad were still together, but that was long ago. Now she felt like her school was too formal and not quite right for her.

Maybe it was because Lorena remembered it so fondly as a child that now it couldn´t compare, but she rather thought that it did come down to the difference in schools between Britain and America, how tiring it was to make new friends when her mother made them move spontaneously and, of course, the lack of having her best friend to walk to school and spend breaks with. She knew Jack so well, even after all these years apart. By the time it took him to answer and by the expression on his face she could tell that he was thinking about how to tell her no.

"You should have fun with your friends", he finally said. "It´s your last big event with them."

"So, we won´t see each other before I leave for America?", Lorena asked, unable to hide her disappointment completely.

"Of course, we will", Jack assured her, leaning closer to the screen. "Just without dancing, dress code and stuff like that."

In that moment, she hated that he made her laugh, even though she wanted to cry.

9

In retrospect, Lorena sometimes wondered what would have happened if she had told Jack then how much she wanted him to be there, how much she wanted him to be part of that day and of everything important in her life, because he was that important of a person to her. She also wondered if he had considered showing up. And whether, if he had, their relationship would have taken a different road altogether. Knowing Jack, that probably had been the very reason concerning him when he turned her down.

"What are you thinking about?"

She raised her head to find Francis looking at her over the clothing rail. Her friend had offered to accompany her dress shopping since she herself also needed a dress for a cousin´s wedding.

Lorena opened her mouth and closed it again, thinking of what to tell her friend. Finally, she took a deep breath, saying: "I applied for a job in our London office. A few weeks back."

Francis raised her brows, but as expected, she didn´t ask for the reason.

"Did you get it?"

"Yes."

The confirmation came this morning.

"Well, congratulations!", her friend said, looking genuinely excited for her.

"Thanks."

"That´s great!"

"Yeah."

Lorena tried to make her voice sound happy, but she didn't quite hit the tone. It wasn't untrue – it was great. She wouldn't have bothered to apply if the idea hadn't resonated with her, but ever since she had gotten the call this morning, she couldn't get herself to feel the excitement she thought she would feel.

"You don't look like it", Francis observed carefully, trying to catch her friend's gaze. "I thought you would be happier about this."

"So did I", Lorena admitted. She could tell that Francis was waiting for an explanation. "I didn't... tell Jack about it."

"Well", Francis said after a moment, reaching for her hand over the rail and squeezing it. "I'm proud of you anyway. And once we have a dress, we will go for a drink and celebrate, okay?"

"Okay", Lorena found herself agreeing with a hint of a smile. "I'll go try this one on."

While she liked to look good and liked to go shopping, on some days Lorena didn't feel like putting on anything fancy. She knew the moment she closed the zipper on the green dress and turned to the in-cabin mirror that this was one of those days.

"I'm not feeling it."

"It's a great color for you though", Francis, who had sat down in one of the chairs before the changing rooms, said. "Maybe we'll find a different one."

Observing her reflection in the mirror, Lorena turned to watch herself from the side. Francis was right about the color and the fitting was flattering as well, summerly airy. It was a decent dress, one her mother would have probably told her to get because one could never own enough classically chic outfits. But her mother would have also told her that she needed a dress she felt confident in, in order to actually look confident. It was one of the few lessons her mother taught Lorena, which she always went by. The green dress wasn´t it.

"So, when do you want to tell him?"

Francis´s voice interrupted her thoughts and Lorena stopped smoothing her skirts.

"Part of me just wants to get it done and call him", she admitted, restarting the gesture. "But part of me thinks this might be a conversation we should have in person."

"Is there much of a conversation to have?"

Lorena furrowed her brows. "What do you mean?"

"Well... I know we never talk about it, but... it`s obvious you love each other. You may not use the words, but surely every single synonym you can think of." Francis hesitated, as she reconsidered her words. "You know what, I take it back. You definitely need to have a conversation about it. Because the only thing keeping the two of you apart is... well, you not a having a conversation."

For the second time today, Lorena glanced at her, considering what to say. They didn´t avoid the topic of Jack entirely, but normally there were no deep inquiries as to her feelings for him. Her friends had long since understood that it was best not to go down that road, but today Lorena didn´t feel her walls come up. Instead, it was the other way around.

"I asked him out once", she admitted, feeling relieved to not be alone with the truth anymore. "He turned me down."

Francis flinched.

"You never said."

The dismay in her voice and face was evident.

"It was embarrassing really", Lorena murmured, looking down at her feet before facing her own reflection. For the last five years, she had repressed that day, this moment of her life, successfully. She was determined to continue to do so.

"You don´t want to make the first move."

It wasn´t a question. Maybe Lorena felt encouraged by her friend´s compassion, maybe she was just tired after all this time. Maybe it was both. But she made one more admission.

"Technically, I also asked him to be my date at prom."

"He´s an idiot", Francis said quietly. "I know you love him, but he really is an idiot."

10

At age ten, Jack was a tall and rather thin boy, who spent most of his time indoors, reading or playing chess. He neither had any ambition to join a sports team nor did he believe that he was physically qualified to play a sport. However, worried about his son, his father signed him up for soccer practice. It turned out, he wasn´t that bad at all. It also turned out, he actually enjoyed it.

11

There was a hissing sound coming from the coffee machine, which was blowing more steam in the air than it probably ought to. A girl with a yellow apron removed it from the power while her coworker took off the lid of the machine, risking a glance. His glasses were foggy within seconds.

"So", Dean said, diverting Jack´s attention back to their table. "When is your dad´s wedding?"

"A little over two weeks."

"He´s really marrying for the fourth time?"

Dean wasn´t unused to an unusually high number of re-marrying. His and Ava´s parents had been together on and off for years, getting married for the third time just one year after their second divorce. They had gotten married to each other though, so there was a difference somehow. Still, due to that fact, Jack knew there was no judgment in the question.

"Yeah", he confirmed, breathing in the word as he removed the teabag from his cup. "Also, I must say I really like Soraya. If they mess things up, I really don´t know what to believe about love anymore."

"Do you have a date?"

"Lorena is flying in from New York", Jack said, aware he was making way for the conversation they had yet to have after his birthday. "My dad suggested it. They kind of always got along." His fingers pounded on the desk. "I think in his way he´s... trying to set us up. At least, that´s what it feels like."

He took a sip from his tea while Dean frowned, adding milk to his own cup. "And you´re not feeling good about that."

In light of recent events, it would have been an easy conclusion, but it sounded more like a question since Dean was still trying to figure out the ground on which he was walking with the subject.

"I don´t know how to... feel about it", Jack admitted. "I know how people see us when we´re together. I know they assume us to be a couple." It was a fact he saw mirrored in Dean´s face, with whom he locked eyes over the table. Dean was listening and Jack hesitated, his eyes moving from his friend to his teacup to the painting on the wall, before he took a deep breath. "I guess the reason I am so sensitive about it is because it´s true. And I don´t want it to be."

It was obvious that Dean still had questions about the relationship, but to his credit, he focused on the matter at hand. "What do you mean?"

"I have been in love with Lorena knowingly for over five years and... unknowingly probably even longer than that", Jack said, surprising himself with the admission. But it felt good to finally say the words out loud, so he continued: "I mean the reason I don´t date is because it´s not fair to anyone to pretend that I am ever going to love anyone more than I love her."

Dean´s eyebrows rose slightly. "Have you ever told her that?"

"Of course not."

"Why?"

"Why?", Jack echoed. "Isn´t that obvious?"

"I think the people that matter will care about your happiness." Dean shrugged. "You can´t change the way people come into your

51

life."

"You don´t find it awkward then?"

"I believe what I said", Dean said, leaning forward. "Jack, you have been really lucky to have found someone you care about so deeply. Don´t throw it away because you´re afraid." Reaching for his cup and leaning back he added: "If you´re not doing it for yourself then do it for Ava. I´m pretty sure she is dying to hang out with Lorena again. Like she won´t shut up about her and New York."

It wasn´t his intention to snort, but it had been Dean´s intention and for all the non-fittingness of the topic change, Jack appreciated breaking up the tone of conversation.

"I might give Ava her number."

"Please do."

"That´s another thing to consider though", he said, as their grinning died down.

"What is?"

"New York. Oxford."

"You´ll figure it out. I mean technically you guys kind of are in a long-distance relationship already."

Jack wasn´t sure whether he agreed with the phrasing, but he did know that a long-distance relationship would never work for him permanently, not a romantic one at least. He had been to New York a couple of times and as much as he had tried to get himself to like it, to think about how it would be to live there, he had always ended at the same conclusion. Though he would move to be with Lorena, he knew he would never be happy there – not in the city, not away from his father and friends. And this inevitably led to the next conclusion:

he couldn´t expect Lorena to do any of the things he wouldn´t do.

"One step after another." Dean looked at him as if he knew his mind was already multiple steps ahead. "She might still turn you down. I don´t think she will, but..."

"Telling her about my feelings before worrying about everything else, got it", Jack finished, before releasing a breath he didn´t know he was holding. "Thank you, though. Really. I appreciate it."

"Always."

12

Lorena's relationship with her mother hadn't always been great. One could assume that they were naturally close since it had always been the two of them, Lorena's father nowhere to be seen. But no, it wasn't like that, at least not when Lorena was younger.

Helene had always been thriving in her career. And while that did not make her a neglectful mother, she had always been independent, not so much a family person as Lorena secretly was. At least, she used to believe that. But then she realized why her mother kept going from man to man, moving them from place to place. She had realized that her mother wanted all the same things she longed for, even though she would never admit it.

It still felt selfish to some degree, this constant change she had to face growing up and it didn't entirely resolve Lorena's resentment about it, but it made her feel closer to her mom. Because in the end what she wanted was the kind of family they had been with Jack and Ted, for herself and her daughter, and Lorena couldn't blame her for that. She couldn't even blame her for it not working out. In fact, she actually admired her mother for being able to trust and try again.

"How's work?", Helene asked, knife in hand, cutting the tomatoes for the salad.

Lorena sat on a chair on the other side of the kitchen counter, watching her mother's fast movements. She had long ago given up on asking her mother to help her prepare meals. The answer was always no.

"Fine", Lorena said, because it was true. She liked her job enough, but she wasn´t as passionate about it that she actually wanted to talk about it outside the office. "Yours?"

"Nightmare." She shook her head. "Sometimes I wonder if they would even manage without me."

"Probably wouldn´t."

"I´m about to go on forced vacation and all I can think about is how much paperwork is going to hit me once I´m back. Maybe I´ll take my laptop."

Lorena forced the corners of her lips to remain in their place.

"I somehow don´t think Robert would appreciate that, Mom."

Helene sighed in resignation.

"You´re probably right."

Robert was a medium-height man around sixty, who had a reddish beard, a small beer belly and always wore sneakers to suits, even in the office. Lorena knew that because they worked for the same marketing firm. Now, it might seem like working with your mother´s boyfriend was nothing she wanted, especially not given her mother´s record in ended marriages and proposals, but it had been in fact Lorena herself who introduced the two.

While Lorena had been in college, her mother had tentatively started her relationship with husband number five (not to be confused with almost-stepdad number five), whom she waited to marry until their third year together. They divorced a year later after she had caught him cheating with his ex. It had been then that she declared to stay single, that she had given love all the chances, but no one needed to marry more than five times. For all the times Lorena hadn´t believed her words on spending some time alone and starting new, this time she had. Looking at her mother then, she had looked tired, and it had occurred to her daughter that risking her heart again and again in hopes of finding the right person had taken a toll on her too.

For all her independence one could assume that Helene was good at being alone. And she did do fine, but it wasn´t what she wanted and she wasn´t quite happy, even though happier than in some of her relationships.

Lorena had been paired up with Robert in a workshop at work and at the end of the day, she waved him goodbye, wishing her mother would have married a guy like him instead of some of the others. It had taken her a couple of weeks to decide, but Lorena had eventually convinced her mother to accompany her to a work function, where she had introduced her to Robert.

Though Helene hadn´t been pleased about being set up, she admitted to liking him and agreed to go out with him by the end of the evening. They had been together ever since. Lorena supposed that the reason they fit so well was because Robert was balancing her mother out, in a way that she didn´t feel was degrading to her career, while she got him to try new things. Also, he never proposed, which for some reason seemed to be a plus in Helene´s books.

"But what am I supposed to do on vacation for two weeks? Lay lazily in the sun, get drunk, go sightseeing?"

"That´s what other people do", Lorena pointed out.

Her mother shook her head and focused back on preparing dinner. Lorena stole a cucumber stick yet to be cut for the salad, while Helene seemed to be somewhere else. Lorena knew better than to interrupt her thoughts. Chewing on the cucumber, she waited, until a moment later, her mother looked at her with a quizzical expression.

"Didn´t you and Jack go to Spain once?"

There it was – the memory she didn´t want to have, entering her mind for the second time in the course of one week.

"Italy actually", Lorena said, recovering quickly. Thankfully, her mother didn´t notice.

"Right", she said. "I was hoping you could recommend me some restaurants."

With that, her mind seemed to lose focus once again and Lorena was left to her own thoughts, slowly but surely drifting away to the Italy vacation which had taken place just a few months after her 21st birthday. *I asked him out once. He turned me down.* As her own words repeated in her head, she kind of wished she had taken her mother up on the offer of a glass of wine.

"Talking about Jack though", Helene suddenly said. "Robert mentioned something about you transferring to London?"

"I don´t know about that yet."

That was the downside of working with your mother´s boyfriend.

"Jack is a nice guy and I like him. You know I like him-"

Lorena felt herself getting defensive. "I´m not sure what you´re getting at."

"I worry about you." Helene sighed at the expression on her daughter´s face and finally laid the kitchen knife to the side. "I´m not stupid, Lorena. I know I´ve never been Mother of the Year. But I love you and I want what´s best for you. I just want you to think this through, before uprooting your entire life for a man. I know what I´m talking about."

There were no words spoken about what she thought of her feelings for Jack and Lorena supposed that that was as close as she would ever come to a blessing from her mother for any kind of man. She would never advise Lorena to move to another country, so it was good that she didn´t require her mother´s permission. Because even though she loved her mother and her friends, it would not be enough to make her stay.

13

16 years ago

When their parents first started fighting, Lorena tried to ignore it. Pressing her little hands over her ears, she buried her face deep in her pillow, hoping for the voices to die down. Even at ten, she knew what raised voices meant and she didn't want it to mean what she feared this time.

That was how Jack found her, cowered under her blanket, cheeks wet from quiet tears. She supposed he also knew what raised voices meant. Jack didn't talk about it though. They never talked about the dooming end of their family and their happy life together and Lorena was glad about it. All Jack did was walk over to her CD player, put in an album he had brought from his room and turn it on loud enough to drown out the voices from downstairs, before climbing into bed next to her. They would lie there, staring at the sticky glowing stars on Lorena's bedroom ceiling until the songs finished playing. Usually, the fighting had finished then too.

14

Lorena was sitting at the kitchen table in front of her laptop, one leg pulled up and like Jack, already wearing pajamas. She seemed so absorbed in her work that she didn´t notice him leaning in the doorframe, watching her. He had picked her up at the airport this morning, but it felt like she had been here longer than mere hours. When someone would look through the window, they would see a young couple, living together. Jack liked the idea of that, simply because he liked her being here, even if she was engrossed in work.

Jack had been ending his second year at college, the first time he realized that she wasn´t just objectively pretty, but that she was pretty to him. That, in combination with the realization that he did like her more than other girls, hit him completely unexpectedly. So, when she spun in her prom dress and asked him to go with her, he rejected her, convinced that by the next time they would see each other, he would have sorted his thoughts, and everything would be normal again. And for a while, he thought it was. Until he came to see her for her 21st birthday. It had been the first time he thought about kissing her.

Jack often thought about kissing her. Not in the time that followed that day. While he thought about the confused state of his feelings, he banished the idea of kissing her from his head. If hugging her could break his heart, he couldn´t possibly hurt himself with a fantasy that would never happen. No, when Jack thought about kissing Lorena, it was always in moments like this, when he realized how comfortable the little things in life could be.

"You look tired."

Her voice broke him out of his thoughts.

"Well, it is almost midnight."

"Not my time", she pointed out.

Jack shoved his hands down his pockets, watching her resume typing for a moment.

"Will you come to bed anyway?"

"Sure. I´ll just finish this."

Jack stayed in place for a moment longer, before pushing himself from the doorframe, returning to his bedroom and squatting down to open the cabinets of the sideboard. Opting for the two most used discs he held them above his head, as he heard Lorena´s footsteps on the floor.

"Any special wishes?", he asked, even though he knew the answer.

"Left, obviously."

The mattress creaked as Lorena threw herself onto the bed. The CD started playing and Jack turned down the volume to a soft background noise.

"Even after all those years, it´s one of the best songs."

Maybe it was weird to enjoy a song one had heard on repeat to drown out their parents´ fights, but Jack shared the sentiment. It was a good song and a good album. He didn´t think of divorce when listening to it, but of lying next to Lorena, sometimes singing along with dramatic gestures, making it their own funny game, so the fights went forgotten.

"Want to keep a reading light on?"

"No, it´s fine."

The room went dark, and Lorena cuddled automatically into Jack´s opened arm, burying her head in his neck, while his arms hugged around her. As the songs played on, she wished time would suspend, allowing them to stay like this forever. She had always wondered how they could be so intimate, acting like a couple while pretending like they weren´t. Lorena only had a short dating history, but she had never been so comfortable with another person. Maybe she never really tried. In a way, they were in a committed relationship with each other without actually being in one. It was a death sentence for every other attempt at a romantic relationship.

The track had stopped playing a while ago. Lorena turned her head a little to see the features of Jack´s face before she spoke into the darkness of the room: "I got offered a job in our London office."

He was quiet for a while before he asked: "Are you going to take it?"

"I don´t know."

The answer, of course, depended on him. She didn´t say, but there was no need to. She knew, he knew, and was proven right by the husky tone of his voice, which he tried to cover up.

"When do you have to decide?"

"Next week. But I wanted to talk to you first."

"You don´t need my permission."

"No", she said, unable to hide her disappointment at the answer. "I suppose not."

"You´re my favorite person. I´d love to see you more often", Jack said softly. "But don´t make this decision based on me. You should do what you want."

"Yeah."

Lorena snuggled into him a little more, well aware that she wouldn´t sleep for a while. Jack hadn´t asked her to stay, not that she had expected him to. But now she had to think about whether she wanted London without him.

15

Ted and Helene broke up on a Monday morning. As they came back from school, Lorena and Jack saw the suitcases in the hallway. There were no raised voices this time, just silence and tight expressions. Lorena's mother hushed her upstairs to pack her things. Jack looked from his father to his friend. Her eyes filled with tears, and she started to cry hysterically, while Helene tried to patiently calm her daughter down. Ted tried to explain and comfort his son. Jack didn´t cry, but for the first time, he felt angry with his father and asked him to let Lorena stay with them. In the end, they had to part ways at the front door.

16

Other than with his friends, Jack never worried about Lorena meeting his family. Or, at least, he never worried about her meeting his dad. Ted was already standing outside, as Jack pulled onto the driveway.

"You know he´s going to give you at least an hour-long tour around the garden, right?"

"And you know I would even let your dad take me on a two-hour-long tour around the *yard*, right?", Lorena said, opening her seatbelt just as Jack turned off the engine. "And before you fight me on this – yes, garden refers to the area where you grow the flowers and plants, but the flower garden is contained *within* the yard."

„Yard is a *unit*", Jack pointed out, but she was already out of the car. Shaking his head he slowly unfastened his seatbelt, his heart warming as he watched his father and Lorena embrace, beaming at each other and chatting excitedly.

The words from the night before had been echoing in his head the entire drive here. Lorena had seemed content with watching the landscape in companionable silence, giving him more time to gaze at her and wonder at the possibility of things always being like this. The possibility of *them*.

"I´m so glad Jack brought you", Ted said, laying his palms on Lorena´s shoulders. "It really has been too long."

"I´m glad too. And excited. Thank you for having me."

Jack still couldn´t wrap his mind around it. It was everything he wanted and yet, he hesitated, doubts and overthinking nagging at him.

He wanted her to stay but was afraid it might be too much to ask.

"Always, darling. Let me get your stuff."

The noise of his father´s footsteps on the gravel brought Jack´s mind back into the present. Ted welcomed him with an embrace, as Soraya made her way onto the driveway, shielding her eyes from the sun as she approached her guests.

"Oh, there you are!", she said, and Jack gave her a short wave, which she returned, before turning to the person closest to her. "Hi, I´m Soraya – you must be Lorena."

The two women shook hands, before exchanging polite kisses on each cheek in some sort of half embrace. What sounded like an awkward greeting, somehow had a sincere friendly notion, which could only be blamed on the natural grace of both parties. Ted turned to his son, raising an eyebrow, and Jack had a hard time containing a smile.

"Nice to meet you. Is that the ring? Oh, it´s beautiful. Ted – I didn´t know you to have such good taste."

He reached to lift Lorena´s suitcase out of the trunk. "Women or jewelry?"

"Ha ha." Soraya rolled her eyes at him, but a conspirational smile remained on her face, as she turned back to Lorena. "Don´t even listen to him – it´s a family heirloom. He had to do quite some convincing to get my mother to give it to him."

"And were she here she would tell you that she still isn´t convinced." Ted placed the suitcase next to the door, his comment earning him a light slap on the arm from his fiancé. "What? It´s true!"

"My mother will be arriving this afternoon for tea already, but she´ll be staying in the nearby hotel, together with Ted´s mum and sisters."

Jack felt his smile drop. "They´re all on their way already?"

"Well, Carol and Abigail wanted to help with preparations tomorrow and you know what your grandmother is like."

While Jack never had to worry about Lorena meeting his father, the rest of his family – especially his grandmother – was a different matter altogether.

Next to him, he could see that the smile on Lorena´s own face had tightened, clearly remembering the last time she had spent time in Gram´s company. She was a woman of many convictions, one of them being that marriage was supposed to be about making a choice and sticking to it. She had never approved of her son´s way of life, nor had she ever liked any of his wives or partners. Helene, however, had been different. Helene, she did not simply disapprove of. No, Helene she downright loathed from the very first moment they met. Maybe because she had a similar track of love affairs as Ted, but most likely because she was a *woman* with a similar track of love affairs as Ted, she became the scale every other partner – past or present – was measured against.

"Well", Soraya said cheerily in an attempt to diffuse the tension. "How about we get this to your rooms, you settle down and then we have a cup of tea before all hell breaks loose?"

"Fantastic idea", Ted agreed readily. "Lorena, we prepared your old room for you. Jack, you´re in your room, of course – I assume you both know the way."

"Sure."

The room Lorena had occupied in their house had stopped looking like her room a long time ago. For Jack, it had been instant. The moment she was gone, the spirit had left the walls, even though the color on them remained the same for at least two more years.

"It looks different", Lorena noted, as she stepped into the white furnished guest room, which had more likeness to an interior design catalog than the pink postered room it had been all those years back.

"Yeah, I guess", Jack said, leaning in the doorframe. As she looked around, he tried not to remember how often his 12-year-old self had stopped in the hallway, staring into the empty room with a ball of emotions boiling up inside of him. Back then, he would have raged if his father had attempted to refurnish, but when he was 14 years old and came home one day to see white buckets of paint and the furniture moved, he didn't say anything. There was only one thing that had remained the same. "But the sticky stars are still there."

Jack glanced up at the ceiling and caught the hint of a smile on Lorena's face, as she did the same.

"Guess no one could ever question *that* interior design choice", she said jokingly, pulling her mouth into a teasing smile, making Jack snort.

There was no time for that cup of tea, because shortly after Jack left for his room and Lorena started unpacking her suitcase, the doorbell rang and the familiar voices of Jack's aunts and grandmother echoed through the house.

Jack appeared in the doorframe, a little hesitant about whether he should ask her to come down. A small smile appeared on her lips, one she knew he could see right through, but she meant her words nonetheless. "I´ll be right with you." She just needed to prepare herself a little.

Normally, Lorena didn´t mind people not liking her. But with Jack and Ted´s family that was different, simply because *they* were different. They were two of the people whom she cherished most in life, and it was only natural to want the people they valued in life to at least not hate her.

After freshening up her face and changing into a light summer dress, Lorena brazed herself and walked down the stairs. The murmur of voices grew louder and clearer, as she took the last step and walked through the hallway.

"I just think it´s weird that he´s still friends with her", Gram´s high-pitched voice sounded from the living room. "Don´t you think it´s weird?"

Lorena stopped in her tracks, hesitating to take the turn to her right into the bright and open room. It wasn´t that she wanted to eavesdrop, but having heard the first part, she could not quite bring herself to face Jack´s family yet.

"I think it´s quite nice Jack has at least gained something from my marriages."

"But still, it is not appropriate for her to be here." Gram paused, considering her words. "Unless, of course, they are sleeping together."

"Mama!"

This time the shocked voice was Abigail´s. Or Carol´s. Lorena honestly couldn´t tell, but she rather suspected that the voice was

Abigail´s, because she didn`t doubt the snickering sound came from Carol. Ted´s younger sister rather took after their mother.

"If they´re sleeping together it would make sense for her to come", Gram insisted, completely ignorant of the reaction she had caused. "Even though that would be quite another level of inappropriate."

"They are not sleeping together", Ted insisted. "They are just friends."

"And how would you know that?"

"Everything alright?"

The sound of Jack´s voice startled her out of listening to words that weren´t meant for her ears.

"Yes", she lied. "All good."

It was obvious from the furrow in his brows that he did not believe her. "Are you sure?"

"Yeah, of course. Let´s go meet your family."

"Alright."

They walked through the door. Jack´s family had already gathered in the middle, sipping on champagne. Upon their arrival, Soraya immediately went to fill two more glasses.

"There you are", Ted said, smiling and waving them closer. "Lorena, you remember my mother and sisters?"

"Of course, nice to see you again."

There were polite smiles from Ted´s sisters, but no attempts at hand shaking or hugging, which she hadn´t expected anyway. Jack´s hand still lay reassuringly on her back from when he had guided her in. Lorena´s body was alarmingly conscious of the touch. Gram´s eyes darted to her grandson´s hand placed on her body, then back to

Lorena´s face, narrowing all so slightly. She was alarmingly conscious of it as well.

"Here you go."

"Thank you", Lorena said, taking the glass from Soraya, welcoming the opportunity to break eye contact with the older woman.

"So, Ted told us that you flew in all the way from America", Carol said.

"Yes, I did."

"Isn´t that a lot of trouble for someone who isn´t even part of your family anymore?"

Jack´s body stiffened noticeably and for a moment, Lorena didn´t know what to say. "Well, I´m not one to question the guest list."

"Of course not, dear", Gram tuned in, her voice even and hollow in that formal way of hers, which surely could challenge the one or other aristocrat. "My daughter just can´t imagine going out of her way for anyone, no matter how close to her."

There was a moment of silence and Lorena noticed Soraya taking a long sip from her glass, clearly bracing herself for a very long afternoon. As she caught her gaze, she hinted at an eye roll and Lorena found herself smiling. Realizing that Gram was once again monitoring her, she attempted to hide her expression by raising her glass to her lips as well.

"Well, I would like to make a toast!" Ted raised his glass and turned to look at each one of them. "To family – old and new."

17

The wedding took place on Friday afternoon on the grounds of the manor, with a little over 100 guests to witness the occasion. Jack was standing next to his father as he said his vows. But while Ted only had eyes for his new bride, his son looked to the third row on the right, at the woman in the light blue dress.

18

The day was uncommonly sunny. In preparing for the normal weather conditions, a huge white tent had been placed in the garden, under which the tables and dance floor had been put up. There was, however, not a single cloud in the sky.

"Looks like we chose a good day."

"Sure does."

Soraya let herself plump into the chair next to Jack, uncaring for possible wrinkles in her white dress. As the star of the occasion, he couldn´t blame her for seeking a quiet moment to process. He had done the same, leaving the tent for the terrace, from which he could observe all the festivities, without actually participating.

"She´s great."

Jack didn´t have to ask who she meant. His eyes had been glued to Lorena all day and were following her even now, as she was laughing carefree and dancing with his father, both of them slightly out of rhythm. It wasn´t surprising Soraya had caught on so fast.

"Yeah, she is."

"You must love her a lot."

"I do", Jack admitted, seeing no reason to deny it.

"Are you going to tell her that?", Soraya asked.

"I don´t know." He turned to look at his stepmother, furrowing a brow as he saw what she was doing. "I thought you quit smoking?"

"I did", Soraya said, pulling a cigarette out of the box anyway. "Want one?"

"No, thanks."

"Better for you. Some motherly advice? I think you should tell her. What do you have to lose?"

Nothing.

Everything.

One moment he thought there was nothing that could destroy his relationship with Lorena. Then it felt like the most fragile thing in the world, about to break at the slightest wrong step.

Jack looked back to the tent, where Lorena and his dad had stopped dancing. She was now chatting and laughing with one of Soraya´s cousins. The dress she was wearing was similar to the one she had worn to prom. The prom he could have gone to with her. Sometimes he wondered what would have happened if he had.

"I´m scared."

Soraya nodded slowly, no humor in her voice as she followed his gaze.

"Me too."

Love was always scary. It said nothing about trust in the relationship. And, Jack realized, getting married to someone who had promised forever to three other women before, was probably even scarier.

"For the record", he said, therefore. "From all of my dad´s wives and girlfriends over the last years – I like you best."

"You´re not so bad either", Soraya said, the corners of her mouth pulling up, before inhaling deeply. "You have a terrible taste in music though – no appreciation for the 80s."

Jack chuckled. "Well, they had some good songs."

"See and that´s where you´re wrong."

Lorena had spotted Jack and Soraya taking some time off the festivities, chatting and clearly enjoying each other's company. For that she was glad. Though he never mentioned it, it had been hard for Jack to get used to the different women in his father's life. He always tried, probably more so than she had with her mother's partners, but they were different people. Lorena welcomed them, without attaching herself too much. It was a quality Jack didn´t possess. It took him time to get used to and comfortable with them and by that time, usually, the women were already gone. Lorena couldn´t recall him mourning after a single one of them, but she knew it was exhausting to him. Seeing Jack and Soraya getting along so well, she felt quite happy for both of them. This was the first part of a happy ending, at the very least for the three of them.

As Jack turned his head, she had already made most of her way over and smiled brightly at the bride, before pointedly holding out a hand to Jack. "Care to dance with me?"

There was a moment of hesitation, in which he looked up at her in awe, before clearing his throat and reaching for Lorena´s hand as he stood. "Sure." As he lightly squeezed her fingers, she felt her chest warm. "Do you mind?"

Soraya waved her hand dismissively. "Go ahead, have fun. I´ll enjoy a few more minutes of peace before I have to play nice with your Gram."

Lorena pulled Jack with her to the dance floor where they started what was supposed to be the Foxtrot. Neither of them could quite manage the right steps. They bumped or missed turns more often than not, but Lorena felt carefree and happy, almost bubbling over with laughter, as the song came to a stop, changing to a slower tone. Still a little dizzy, Jack had to steady her before she could trip.

"You good?"

"I´m fine."

The corners of his lips were pulled up in the way that she liked, lighting up his beautiful face. She started to lift her hands to touch it but caught herself in time. There was no indication he noticed. His eyes were still fixed on hers. When he pulled her in for a slow dance, Lorena allowed herself to rest her head on Jack´s shoulder and close her eyes.

They were more hugging than dancing and she forced herself to relish the feeling that came with living in the moment, knowing their time was almost up again and their future uncertain. He rested his head on hers. Lorena wondered if Jack knew how much she was hurting and if he was trying to comfort her. Sometimes Lorena contemplated how much easier her life would be if she could just let go of her feelings for him. She never managed it though. Maybe that was her tragedy.

"I don´t want you to leave."

Lorena pulled back her head, her eyes searching his face. "What?"

She half expected the words to leave his mouth to be different ones, that somehow, she misheard.

"I don´t want you to leave", Jack repeated, his eyes serious and steady on hers.

Her lips parted, but before words could form, the music broke off and the screeching sound of the microphone forced the wedding guests to turn their attention to the stage. Lorena, too, took a step back and made herself look away from Jack, hoping it would help to clear her head. Yet, she couldn´t comprehend.

"I believe it is time for me to throw my bouquet - what do you say?" Soraya smiled at her guests and a few of them started cheering and clapping. "Amazing. If all my girls could come a little closer – I´m not sure how high I can lift my arms in this dress and I know for a fact my husband would hate for these flowers to get smacked on the ground, so..."

There was a low echo of laughter, but Lorena couldn´t bring herself to join and as she turned back, Jack wasn´t laughing either. The look her gave her hinted at concern, but his voice didn´t betray his feelings.

"You heard the bride", he said, nodding to the middle of the space, where a group of female guests had already formed.

If this were one of the romance movies Lorena watched with her friends on girls´ night, the bouquet would have landed right in her arms or at her feet, and she would have had to dance a slow romantic dance with Jack while everyone watched. This wasn´t a movie however and Lorena was glad that the bouquet was caught by one of Soraya´s friends from school, whom she had shortly talked to earlier. Not having to dance, though, meant having to stand at the edge of the dance floor, with Jack right beside her. Being double aware of every breath he did, every movement he made, Lorena had a hard time not turning around to where she could feel him standing way too close to her.

Feeling suddenly overwhelmed, her heart racing, Lorena took the first opportunity after the dance to excuse and push herself through the tight gathering of people, she felt were like walls trying to cut off her oxygen. She took a deep breath, as she made her way across the lawn with short, hurried steps. There was, luckily, no one inside, so she could enjoy a moment of peace to calm herself down.

"Are you okay?"

Of course, Jack had come after her. On every other day, in every other moment, his care would have been sweet. Right now, she found herself sounding annoyed.

"I´m fine", she lied.

"You don´t look fine", Jack said, hesitating for a moment. "Is it because of what I said? We can forget I said anything if it makes you uncomfortable-"

"It´s not about that", she snapped, feeling a pang of guilt at the look on his face at her reaction. It was so easy to be understood by Jack that she sometimes had to remind herself that he could indeed not read her mind or her feelings. He couldn´t know where her sudden irritation came from. He could assume, but he could not really know. She took a deep breath, sounding more collected, as she added: "Well, maybe a little."

It was a nagging suspicion. It didn´t make sense though. She had wanted Jack to ask her to stay when she told him about her job offer. Even though he didn´t ask then, she should be happy he had asked her now. Still, she couldn´t help feeling frustrated and exhausted, with the back and forth. She had started to come to terms that he wouldn´t ask and that she would have to, once and for all, accept that he never would. But now he had and she wasn´t able to process that information. Neither mentally nor emotionally.

Jack frowned. "So-"

Lorena was not supposed to find out what he was about to say, because his new stepmother chose this very moment to stumble into the living room, carrying a somewhat weird-looking statue wrapped with a white bow tie.

"Don´t even ask", she said, putting it down and letting her gaze slide through the room. "I have no idea what it´s supposed to be and I´m too sober to even try to guess. But your father´s friend tried so it will probably end up standing here *somewhere*."

"Maybe next to the plant tree", Lorena suggested. "The one by the window?"

"That actually looks cute", Soraya admitted, after adjusting the wedding gifts position a little. "Okay, I have to get back and tell Ted where I put it in case his friend asks."

Lorena didn´t know what to say. She waited for Jack to fill the silence with the words he had wanted to say just a moment earlier. As he opened his mouth, the terrace door slid open once more and one of the bridesmaids kicked off her heels before heading towards the toilets.

"Maybe let´s talk upstairs", Jack suggested.

As an answer, Lorena turned towards the hallway. The silence weighed heavy on her, the feeling in her stomach was like slipping off the top of a rollercoaster. She kept her hands close to her body, reaching for her arms, as soon as the railing was gone, scared that they might start shaking.

"I really like Soraya.“

"Yeah, she´s great", Jack agreed. "Do you think there´s any chance your mother will marry Richard?"

"I don´t see them breaking up. But I don´t think they will marry." Lorena took a deep breath. „But that is not what we wanted to talk about.“

„No. It is not.“

A thought shot through Lorena´s mind as she took the time to just look at Jack, into the grey eyes that looked at her the way she imagined she looked at him as well – like the familiarity of the other person actually made them a part of oneself. But maybe, they wouldn't get married either. Maybe for them, time had finally worn out. Maybe this, right here, was the end.

For the second time today, Jack surprised her as he took a step forward, then another, until he was standing in front of her, close enough to touch her cheek with his right hand, fingers trembling all so slightly. Lorena´s heart beat so loudly in her chest that it drowned out the world around them.

Time seemed to stop as Jack pressed a soft kiss against her lips. His eyes seemed to be overflowing with feelings and thoughts, mirroring her own overwhelmed state. But among them was something else, the uncertainty if this had really been okay. Lorena couldn´t change that this was a momentous occasion, a turning point in their relationship. But she could take his fear away.

Lorena pushed herself up on her toes and kissed him. A feeling of contentedness washed over her, as he pulled her into his arms and held her there.

19

That feeling lasted less than a day. At brunch the next morning, where the closest family of bride and groom were in attendance, they were gushing about the wedding and Soraya´s father was the one who took a look at the couple sitting opposite him, making the remark that would trigger the beginning of the end.

"Next wedding will be yours, I assume", he smiled, unaware of the way all but him, his wife and Gram paused mid-movement. No one could fault him and Lorena took too much of a liking to Soraya´s parents to do so, but at that moment her stomach dropped multiple stories.

Jack´s grandmother snorted: "Not if I can help it", and took a sip from her champagne.

"Mum", mumbled Abigail and gave her head a slight shake, while Carol tried to hide her grin behind her own glass. Soraya´s parents looked a little confused at the reaction and Lorena tried to smile at them politely, taking a sip of her own glass to occupy herself.

"Lorena is my third wife´s daughter", Ted chimed in, throwing a smile in their direction. "Jack and her are just friends."

The words somehow made her feel worse. Because in that moment Lorena realized that other than her mother, Ted truly and genuinely believed the words as he said them. She was thinking of an affirmative lie to keep the peace, but she couldn´t think of one, so she continued to smile. The expression on her face shifted to surprise, as she felt the warm touch of Jack´s hand on her skin, as he covered her hand, which was lying on the table, with his. Out of the corner of her eyes, she could see Gram´s glass stopping mid-air. Jack gave her hand a squeeze and cleared his throat.

"Actually", he said, turning to face his family. "We are... kind of together."

Lorena squeezed his hand back, unable to hide the happiness she felt at that moment, her chest feeling like it might overflow with love.

The "How lovely!" coming from Soraya´s mother, who clapped her hands together in genuine delight, got mixed up with bitterly muttered "I knew it", from Jack´s grandmother. Lorena felt the corners of her lips fall.

"We are very happy for you", Soraya said from her place next to Ted, who was sitting at the end of the table, not saying anything.

"Oh, don´t speak for us", Gram muttered. "I am not happy. I told you this would happen, but no one ever listens to me!"

"Mum", Abigail pleaded. "Don´t. Please."

"This is inappropriate", she continued, ignoring one daughter, while the other looked like she was highly entertained by the developments. "But what was to be expected after that girl was raised by a mother who has such a lack of respect for propriety and the concept of marriage in and of itself. In my days, we had a word for that, young lady. And we have a word for you too."

Lorena flinched at the venom in her voice.

"Don´t talk to her like that", Jack said and, in that moment, she couldn´t help but feel bad for him. Though the words were meant to wound her, having a person you cared about say them was probably worse. "It´s not okay, Gram."

"You´re such a smart boy, you should know better. Back in my days, this would have been incest."

After that, no one said anything.

"Mhm, these are really good", Abigail murmured halfheartedly, taking a bite from her fruit. "Where did you get them?"

"Market", Soraya said, obviously too stunned to engage in small talk about fruit. Gram rammed her fork into hers and continued as if nothing had happened.

Jack looked at her, as Lorena pulled her hand from under his. Her voice sounded hollow in her own ears as she said: "I think I should go."

Jack looked from her to his father and Lorena also made the mistake of looking at Ted, who still hadn´t moved. His face was unreadable and he couldn´t look at either of them. "That´s probably best."

Lorena only hesitated for a second before she pushed herself off the table and stood. Her lips were tingling and her hands felt cold and sweaty. Though she felt like running, she walked out calmly, with as much composure as she could muster. It wasn´t until she had reached the hallway leading to the stairs that she felt her feet moving quicker, hurrying her up the steps into her room.

It didn´t take long for Jack to follow her there. He looked a little lost, standing in the doorframe, watching her. "What are you doing?"

His voice was like that of a little kid, making her feel closer to crying again after she had just convinced herself she could pull through. She hated this for him even more than for herself.

"Packing", she said, trying to sound lighthearted. "My flight leaves in a couple of hours and I have to get all the way back."

Throwing the last few items inside her suitcase, she felt Jack monitoring her movements. "Do you want me to drive you?"

"No, I... I got myself an Uber."

It took her two attempts to close the suitcase halfway and she flinched, as Jack reached forward to help her. She immediately felt bad and he took a step back. Pulling at the zipper, she managed to close it in one try.

"They just... need some time", Jack said in an attempt to save the situation. "It´s a lot to take in."

Lorena covered her hands with her face and took a deep breath. "We´re not subtle, Jack. If the last years are any indication. Time won´t fix this."

There was no need to tell him about the conversation she had overheard two days ago. The only person that hadn´t known was Ted, and based on his reaction, his feelings on the matter weren´t much more positive.

"My dad will come around", he said, but she could hear the doubt in his voice. "And for the rest... I don´t care for their approval."

"I do", Lorena shrugged, hating the truth behind her words. "I used to believe that I don´t, but I do. Because they are your family, and I want them to like me." She could feel the tears burning behind her eyes again. She took a shaky breath to calm herself. "I always thought, I wanted you to choose me. But not if it means choosing against your family."

Jack looked at her through puppy eyes. "You´re my family."

"I´m not staying, Jack."

For the first time in her life, she was glad for the ocean between them. If she had to stay to see him now, she couldn´t take it. Less than a day after finally being with the man she loved, she had ripped both of their hearts out and shattered them into a million pieces.

No longer able to hold in her tears, she wiped them away with the back of her hand in a swift movement she knew he noticed anyway. He still looked like he was processing her words, unable to find some of his own.

A notification popped up on Lorena´s phone. She looked at it for a heartbeat, before lifting her suitcase from the bed and straightening her dress with her hands, throwing a quick glance in the mirror next to the bed. Then she straightened her shoulders and looked at Jack, who was blocking her way outside the room.

"I guess this is goodbye."

She had a hard time looking at him. After what felt like an eternity, but was probably mere seconds, he lowered his gaze to his feet, before meeting her eyes again.

"Will you call me when you land?"

Lorena forced a smile on her face. Her first instinct was to walk over and wrap her arms around him. But knowing she would be unable to let him go, she pushed herself up on her toes instead and kissed him on the cheek.

"Tell Soraya it was really nice to meet her."

20

8 years ago

"Don´t you think it´s a little early for ice cream?", Jack asked, as Lorena dragged him along. "It´s March."

"It´s never too early for ice cream", she said, shooting him a playful glance over the shoulder as she hopped in line. "I thought I taught you that - Hi, I will have a cup of strawberry and my grumpy companion will have a chocolate mint in a cone."

The corners of Jack´s mouth pulled up in amusement and maybe a little bit of positive surprise that she still remembered which ice cream he liked.

"Grumpy friend?"

"Would *ex-stepbrother slash ex-best friend, who just criticized my ice cream taste* suit you better?" Lorena inclined her head. "Or I could just call you my ex – would probably be shorter."

Jack snorted. "Forget I even asked."

"Thanks." Lorena beamed as she took the cup and cone from the shop guy, before turning and offering Jack the chocolate mint one. "Here you go."

"Thanks."

"You´re welcome."

They walked to sit on the steps in front of one of the larger buildings, where some university students were also enjoying the first bit of sunlight this year. Like him, they wore normal clothes, other than Lorena, who was still in her school uniform, as she had hurried to take the first train out of London after classes ended. She didn´t seem the least bit bothered by it and Jack felt himself reminded of all the times they used to sit together like this as kids. It wasn´t the same anymore. The girl next to him was a stranger, someone he once knew better than himself.

"So, I´m your ex-best friend, hm?", he asked, breaking the silence between them. "Should I be offended?"

"I was just trying to prove a point", Lorena said. "You are certainly my eldest friend, my most trusted one as well, so I guess you have a good chance of getting an upgrade soon. But not too soon. I have to account for the years we didn´t talk in a reasonable way."

"That´s what you call reasonable?"

"Are you questioning me?"

"You could have called or written." Jack surprised himself with the words and he could see the humor disappear from Lorena´s face. It bothered him, he realized, the lost years. Because in the end, the real loss of their parents´ divorce had been their friendship. "But I guess, I could have done that too."

"Well, we have obviously learned our lesson, haven´t we?"

21

Jack didn´t go after her. He didn´t go to look outside the window to see her drive away. What he did do was sink to the edge of the bed and bury his face in his hands. Tears were prickling behind his eyes, but they wouldn´t come. There was the sound of tires on the gravel outside. Falling back onto the mattress, he had no idea how much time had passed until he rubbed his eyes and gazed at the ceiling. The annoyance he felt at the sight of the sticky stars was enough to get him to move.

Jack was steeling himself for a fight with his family, but as he walked through the living room and outside, he was surprised, yet relieved, to see that everyone except Soraya, who was clearing the table, was gone.

"I send everyone back to the hotel", she said, as if reading his thoughts and coming over with motherly concern, placing a hand on his arm. "Are you okay?"

"Not really", Jack admitted.

"Could you please tell me what just happened?"

Instead of concerned, Ted looked rather irritated and angry, as he came onto the terrace, arms placed on his hips. Seeing that, Jack couldn´t bring himself to humor him.

"I thought that was rather obvious."

"Well, if it was that would mean that you and Lorena are a couple and that you haven´t mentioned anything indicating that you and her were in a relationship."

"We´re not", Jack answered truthfully, hating that his first instinct was feeling like he had to defend himself. "I don't... I don't know, okay?"

"No, it's not okay", Ted said. "You should have told me."

"I thought you knew. I thought that's why you wanted her to come."

"Ted, I don't want to start a fight on our first day as a married couple", Soraya intervened. "But seriously – are you blind?"

"Excuse me?"

"Dad", Jack said. "You and Helene broke up a decade ago. You've been divorced from her for 16 years for Christ's sake!"

"Jack, I-"

"I love her. And as much as I want you to approve, I will not let you badmouth our relationship or friendship, or whatever it is that is going on between us", he interrupted his father, finally allowing himself to get angry. "I have been nothing but supportive of every one of your relationships. I always tried for your sake, no matter how I felt about it and I quite frankly expect you to do the same for me now. *Especially*, since this is Lorena we're talking about."

"I'm just surprised, Jack", his father sighed, combing his fingers through his hair. "Even though I suppose I probably shouldn't be."

There were many things Jack could have told him, but, as he looked at his father, he didn't feel like saying anything at all. He, too, was just tired of all this. Tired, disappointed, and simply put, done fighting this fight and having to justify himself.

"I'm going to go now."

"I'm sorry", Ted said. "For reacting in a way that gave you the impression I wouldn't approve. Of course, I do."

It wasn't that Jack didn't believe him. He did. But the words could not erase his reaction and right now, they could not conciliate him.

"Yeah, you should probably tell Lorena that", he mumbled, before turning to Soraya. "Sorry for the drama. I didn´t plan to ruin this day for you."

"Oh no, don´t apologize, dear", Soraya said, patting his arm. "Nothing is ruined. Your dad and I will take care of everything here and you go get yourself on the next plane." She gave her husband a pointed look. "Isn´t that right, darling?"

"Of course."

22

5 years ago

The summer after her 21st birthday, Lorena and Jack traveled to Italy. It was one of the best times. They spent all the days together, riding bikes, swimming and venturing through the streets and all nights too, staying up late laughing, drinking wine or sometimes just laying quietly next to each other, looking up at the real stars.

That night, Lorena was already outside, lying in the grass as he lay down next to her, folding his hands on his stomach.

"Do you ever wonder why they didn´t make it?"

She was talking about their parents.

"Not really, no", he admitted, turning his head to the side. "You?"

"It wouldn´t change anything, so it doesn´t matter", she shrugged. "But yeah, sometimes I wonder what our lives would have been like."

"You probably wouldn´t have moved back to America."

"We would probably live in the same city."

"Imagine."

They both chuckled.

"Do you think we would still be friends?", Lorena asked, turning her head to face him.

Jack frowned. "Why wouldn´t we be friends?"

"I don´t know." She turned her head back to the stars. "Maybe we would be more like siblings than friends."

This night´s constellation reminded him of the one in her old bedroom at their house.

"Siblings can be friends."

He knew why she had asked, but he didn´t know what to say. Just like earlier, when they had talked about their unsuccessful dating lives, and she had jokingly suggested that maybe the two of them should go out sometime. They had both laughed, but then she had said that she was serious, that maybe it wasn´t such a bad idea. He hadn´t found the right words then either.

"Lorena?"

She turned to look at him. "Mhm?"

"I love you", Jack said.

"I love you, too."

"Are we okay?"

"Of course", she said, reaching for his hand and squeezing it. "We´re okay."

23

Jack hated flying. Some people liked to do it for vacation or commutation, and he quite frankly thought they had all lost their minds. On their flight to Italy Lorena had tried to argue with him that planes were the safest method of transportation, that the problem obviously was the lack of control one felt when sitting on a plane compared to a car. When he had looked at her, she had been smart enough to shut up.

Jack squeezed his eyes shut, as an air hole let the plane drop a couple of meters. His fingers dug deep into the arms of his seat and there was no way he would dare to take his seatbelt off before they were on safe ground again. That, however, took a lot longer when one couldn´t relax on a plane and even more so when one was in a hurry, but unable to change the time schedule.

There had been no possibility for Jack to get on Lorena´s flight. After leaving his father´s house he had to get his passport and fill out an ESTA application, so he would be able to enter the country. Approval could take up to 72 hours. Jack had driven to the airport anyway, hoping the process would be closed by the time he got there. In the end, he took a flight the next day, which got him to New York around 4 pm local time. This meant that even though he had no suitcase to wait for, it was already 5.38 pm by the time he climbed the stairs to the floor of Lorena´s apartment. He knocked before he could think about it for too long.

It wasn´t Lorena who opened the door.

"Hi."

"Hi", Francis said, blocking the entry with her body, looking slightly like she was ready to shut the door in his face. "Took you long enough."

"British citizens need a visa for the US", Jack said.

She wrinkled her nose, but took a step back from the door so he could enter. "I guess that is fair enough."

In the living room, Lorena's two other friends from college were clearing the small table. The kitchen looked like a mess as well.

Francis closed the door behind him. "You remember Barb and Jenn?"

"Sure", Jack said, returning the polite smile of both women. It had been a while since he last saw them in person, but he knew their faces well from Lorena's social media page and the occasional video call they guest-starred on. Still, the pink in Barbara's otherwise reddish hair irritated him for a moment. "Sorry. Is Lorena here?"

Francis went on to fold the blanket on the couch. "She is not."

"She's taking a walk", Jennifer chimed in, passing the dirty dishes on to Barbara, who went back to take care of the chaos in the kitchen.

"Yeah", she agreed. "We're here because we were worried and trying to cheer her up, but... I don't think she was really feeling it."

"Okay, thanks", Jack said, placing his backpack next to the front door. "Do you mind if I leave my stuff here?"

"Where are you going?"

"To go talk to her. Obviously."

Francis blinked. "But you don't even know where she went."

"Yeah, maybe it's better you wait here", Jennifer said. "We can make you a cup of tea."

Jack shook his head. "Thanks, but I´ll take my chances."

Lorena´s recollection of the last two days was a blur. She was overwhelmed with emotions to the point she stopped processing them altogether. A ghost of herself, she had functioned on autopilot until she had arrived at her apartment yesterday evening. If not for her phone ringing over and over again, waking her from her trance, she probably would have remained on the exact place of the couch where she had sat down after coming home. She hadn´t even taken off her coat by the time her phone started ringing for the fifth time, Jenn´s name illuminating the screen.

When she picked up the call, she could hear the relief on the other end of the line. She hadn´t answered any of her friends since the wedding ceremony and had forgotten to text them after landing as well. Lorena shrugged off her coat, as her friend told her that they´d been worried. All she got was a hollow apology. Jenn asked if she was okay, and Lorena said she didn´t want to talk about it. There was no doubt she was concerned, but she didn´t press the matter after Lorena reassured her that she didn´t need her friends to come over. And they did not come over that evening, but the next day when she opened her door and Francis, Barb and Jenn were standing there, she started to cry. Lorena hated crying. She almost never cried, but when she did, she was on the edge of becoming hysterical. This time was no different. She probably cried for an hour before managing the first coherent sentence as to what had happened. She wasn´t a pretty crier either. But her friends held and comforted her until she was a little calmer and ready to talk. They stayed the entire day. Ted called, Jack didn´t. Barb, the only one of them who was actually good at cooking, made dinner over which Lorena grew more quiet, telling her friends she needed some fresh air. That was where she was now. Sitting on a park bench, wishing she could keep her mind from thinking.

There was the sound of footsteps on the gravel, approaching her. Jack wasn´t smiling as he looked down at her, hands buried in the pocket of the black coat she had talked him into last year.

"Thought I mind find you here."

The coat had been a good choice, she thought. He looked handsome in it.

Lorena figured that he was probably waiting for her to say something, but she couldn´t think of anything.

"Want to walk a little?", Jack asked.

Lorena hesitated but got up eventually. They walked in silence for a couple of moments, before she cleared her throat, breaking it.

"I´m sorry. For leaving the way I did. I just needed some space, I guess."

"It´s okay", Jack said softly. "It´s been an overwhelming few days.“

"Your dad called earlier."

"He did?"

"He wanted to apologize."

Jack nodded slowly but didn´t look at her. "Did you accept?"

The words or lack thereof had hurt. Lorena felt like she was entitled to some sort of grudge, but she also wasn´t petty. She knew she would forgive Ted eventually, so there was no need to fight until then.

"I did. Wasn´t so much into small talk with him though."

"Can´t blame you." Jack turned his head to look at her. "Will you

96

forgive me, too?"

Lorena turned her head and frowned. "What do I need to forgive you for?"

"For not being clear in what I wanted. I should have told you that I wanted you to stay the moment you mentioned moving to London." He shrugged. "It just felt unfair to ask, I guess."

"Why?"

"Because you would never ask me to."

"That´s different", she said.

"How is that different?"

Despite herself, she almost felt like laughing. For people so intimate and close, they really were terrible at talking about their feelings.

"Jack, we´re two very different people", she started to explain. "You always had one home, one place and I never did. It´s not that I wouldn´t miss my friends, but... New York is not my home. Oxford is. You are." She shoved her hands deeper down her pockets. "Besides – you weren´t asking, I was offering."

"We´re really going to fight on the terminology?"

She shrugged helplessly. "If we have to."

His hand closed on her arm, gently forcing her to stop and look at him.

"I love you. I am *in love* with you", Jack clarified. "I´m sorry it took me so long to say it."

Instead of answering, Lorena leaned in and wrapped her arms around him, burying her head in his shoulder. The first time they had talked about love they had been kids. She had been nine years old.

She had been upset after a girl at school had pushed her from her bike and she had scratched open her palms. Jack had taken her to the girls' washroom, cleaning the wound while telling her that she didn´t need to cry because of a mean girl she didn´t even like, because she had a family that loved her – her mother, his father and him too. Though the kind of love was different now, the core of the sentence was still true.

"I´m in love with you, too", Lorena said and closed her eyes as his arms wrapped a little closer around her.

24

Until it really was time to move to Oxford, another three months passed. Lorena had to sign her new work contract, get a working visa and have all of her stuff shipped. What first appeared to be a very long time, ended up being no time at all.

"I think we all knew that you would eventually leave us", Francis said, as she hugged her friend goodbye at the airport. "But I am really happy for you."

"Thank you", Lorena said, holding her friend tighter. No matter how sure she was about this, a part of her still hated saying goodbye. "I will visit of course."

"You better will."

Next in line was her mother, who had already dipped away a tear or two, when she thought no one was looking. Not that she would have been the only one. Barb had been trying to calm Jenn down for the past ten minutes. "Take care, sweetheart. Call me when you land."

"I will", Lorena promised as she let go of her mother.

Helene snorted as Richard gave her a new handkerchief but took it anyway to carefully wipe her eyes. "If we draw this out any longer, I will ruin my make-up."

Lorena rolled her eyes, but still reached in for a last hug with everyone, shedding a couple of tears of her own.

The airport was uncommonly empty due to the early hour, with the lights in the waiting hall still too bright and reflecting off the white tiled floor surface. Jack checked his phone for a text from Lorena and smiled as he read: *Landed :)*

The bundle of flowers in his hand looked a little disarranged from the drive. Ted probably would have had a heart attack at the sight of the poor plants, but there was nothing Jack could do about it now, other than rearranging them a little so the ones hanging their heads were at least lightly supported by the surrounding flowers.

Jack tried to stifle his laugh but failed, as he saw Lorena from afar, pushing one big suitcase to either side of her. Her hair was pulled up in a bun, a hairstyle that suited her very well. He decided he needed to tell her more often. Besides that, with her beige trousers and the black turtleneck, she looked almost as casual as she would ever dare to leave the house. Maybe even she drew the line at overnight flights.

As Lorena noticed him, she grinned. "Last chance to change your mind, my friend."

"I brought you flowers", Jack said, giving the colorful bundle to her, causing them to rearrange and two on the sides to drop their heads. "You still can turn around, too, I guess."

"Not a chance. You are stuck with me now."

Jack pulled her in for a tight hug, before cupping her cheeks with his hands and kissing her. Seeing the blush on her cheeks, his lips curled into a grin, earning himself a nudge in the side.

He pointedly held out his hand for her. "Ready?"

"Sure", she said, taking it.

Together, they made their way towards the exit and onto the parking lot to Jack´s old car. The suitcases, impressively, fitted into the trunk without problems.

"I might need to warn you", Jack said, closing the driver's door beside him. "I think Ava is throwing a welcome party for you."

Epilogue

Two years after Lorena slightly freaked out about looking a mess for arriving at her own welcome party, where she enjoyed herself with Jack´s friends anyway, the two of them got married. Both their families were in attendance and their friend groups merged into one as if they had known each other for years. The best speech was held by Dean, the best man, who talked about friendship and true love, closely followed by Ava, whose ironic storytelling skills made her brother roll her eyes, but everyone else double over with laughter. Ted and Helene brought out the presentations Jack and Lorena had made when they were children.

The words in American and British English may differ based on pronunciation or spelling. They may also be different vocabularies altogether. It can be said that in the course of their life together, Jack and Lorena fought about every single one of them.